CAT'S WITCH
and the
WIZARD

TIGER series

Kara May

CAT'S WITCH
and the
WIZARD

Illustrated by Doffy Weir

Andersen Press · London

For Herman

Text © 1993 by Kara May
Illustrations © 1993 by Doffy Weir

First published in 1993
by Andersen Press Limited,
20 Vauxhall Bridge Road, London SW1V 2SA.
This edition published 2002.

British Library Cataloguing in Publication Data available
ISBN 0 86264 471 2

Phototypeset by Intype, London
Printed and bound in China

1

Cat lived with a witch whose name was Aggie. His witch had size 17 feet. Just now, these size 17 feet were sploshing about in a puddle.

'Get out of
there, Aggie!
At once!'
said Cat. 'You're
muddy all over!'
   'A little mud
never hurt anyone!
I like a good splash!'
laughed Aggie.
   Cat sighed. How
he wished his witch
would behave like
a lady, or at least
a grown-up!

'Now what's she up to?'

His witch was now standing on tip-toe, looking over the hedge of a smart bungalow.

'Where are your manners?' he hissed. 'That's rude.'

'It's not rude to spy on The Enemy! It's common sense! The more we know about him, the better.'

'The Enemy' was Wizard Wesley Wenzil, or Wesley as he liked to be called. He was a newcomer to Wantwich, the town where Cat lived with his witch.

Since he'd arrived the
Wantwichers had gone to him
when they needed magic. For
three full months, Aggie Witch
and Cat hadn't had a customer,
not one. Their money-box was all
but empty.

Cat leapt up onto the hedge.
There were times when manners
must take second place! And this
was one of them, he thought.

'Let me look, Aggie! My eyes
are better than yours!'

Just then, the front door opened. In the doorway stood the Wizard himself. 'What can I do for you?' he asked.

'You can pack up your bags and clear out! Now! At once! You've put me out of business,' said Aggie.

'It's not my fault the Wantwichers come to me and not you!'

9

'More fool them! At least I look like what I am! A witch! You look like the manager of a supermarket! And a cut-price one at that!'

Cat's red eyes sparked. 'You haven't even got a cat! You ought to be struck off the Wizard List!'

The Wizard gave a pleased-with-himself smile. 'Tall hats and cloaks and even magical cats are things of the past. Today belongs to technology. But I don't want to fall out with you. Come on in for a cuppa!'

Aggie winked at Cat. It would

be a chance to look round. 'A
cuppa would go down a treat.
Don't mind if I do!' she said.

They followed the Wizard into
the bungalow. It was computers
and gadgets, wall to wall.

'I keep all my spells on this!'
The Wizard held up a disk. 'It
takes up less space than books.'

'You don't need a screen to read a book. You can read it wherever you like. You can keep your disk what's it!' said Aggie. She took a sniff from the test tube beside her. 'Phew! What a pong! It smells like bats' legs.'

'That's just what it is!' said the Wizard. 'And here we have spiders' brains! And this here is beetles' wings! With the aid of my brains and computers, I've worked out the chemical formulas. It's not so messy as real creepy crawlies. People prefer it.'

'Hold it! Right there!'

Aggie pointed to the small bag he was about to put into a mug.

The Wizard laughed. 'It won't hurt you, Aggie. It's a tea-bag.'

'I don't drink tea from bags. You never know what's in them. I like my tea made from leaves, in a pot. And a china pot at that! Come, Cat. Let us not detain Mr

13

Tea-Bag any longer.'

Aggie wrapped her cloak
grandly around
her and swept
out.

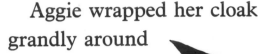

'There! How about that, Cat! I
can act hoity-toity like a lady
WHEN I WANT TO. But right
now, I want –' Aggie broke off as

14

a crowd of Wantwichers came round the corner. At a glance, she could tell that something was wrong. 'Cross your fingers, Cat, we could be in business!' She strode up to the Mayor who was walking in front.

'Morning, Ms Mayor. What's up? You look very green around the gills.'

The Mayor gave an icy look. 'I

do not have gills! I am not a fish!'

'Fish or not, you're a sickly green. In fact, you all are!' said Aggie, scanning the crowd of Wantwichers. 'What's the problem? Whatever it is, I'm your witch. I'll sort it out.'

'The problem is my dad keeps throwing up,' piped up little Ali Shah. 'He's been throwing up ever since he started work at the factory. And so has everyone else.'

Aggie knew the factory he meant. There was just one in Wantwich, a new factory, Teknik Electronics. The Wantwichers had welcomed it, for work in the town was hard to find and now there were jobs for all.

'I've not been there as yet,' said Aggie. 'Which side of town is it on? This or the other?'

'The other, where the wood
used to be. Not that I went there
much,' said Ali. 'It made my dog's
hairs stand up like a brush.'

'That will do, Ali,' said the
Mayor. 'Aggie doesn't want to
know about that.'

'Oh yes I do!'
snapped Aggie.
'The more I know,
the quicker I can
find out what's
wrong and
put it right.'

'We don't *want* you to put it right,' retorted the Mayor. 'We want the Wizard.'

'But that's not fair! I was here first,' screeched Aggie. 'You mean ungrateful creatures! After all I've done for you!'

'That's right, Aggie! You tell them!' said Cat.

'And it's not just me!' Aggie raged on. 'Cat risked his life to get the monster out of the lake. Now all I can afford to feed him is scraps!'

'That's your business not ours. Our business is the Wizard. Now let us pass. We're in a hurry,' said the Mayor. 'Until what's wrong is put right at the factory, we can't work. And work means money!'

'Don't I know it! But I'm not one to beg,' said Aggie. 'If you don't want your witch, see if I care!'

She turned and walked off down the lane, with her head held high. However, once indoors, she slumped into her chair. 'How much money have we got, Cat?' she asked.

Cat emptied the money-box.

'Five pounds,' he said.

'Five pounds between us and

starvation. If we don't get some
work-money soon, we'll have to
leave Wantwich and find a town
where people want us. If there is
such a town!' said Cat's witch
Aggie.

2

Aggie and Cat sat on the chimney pot. They liked to sit there when the sun was out, and look out over the town and far around.

'I wonder how often we'll sit here again,' said Aggie. 'This is the only house I've ever had in all my hundreds of years of life. It'd break my heart not to live in it.'

Aggie gave a sigh so sad that Cat's whiskers trembled. He hadn't wanted to live in a house at first. But now he'd be as sorry as his witch to leave. He glowered at the Wantwichers still gathered around the Wizard's bungalow. 'I hope his computers go berserk, turn them into synthetic toads, and then his lasers zap them!'

'Never fret, Cat. If we have to leave our dear little Roof Hole House, the Wantwichers will

know about it and wish they
didn't. But it's not come to that!'

Aggie got to her feet and gave a
soft whistle.

At once the broomstick flew up
through the hole in the roof.

'On you get, Cat. I want to find
out what's what at the factory.
I've a feeling in my bones there
could be money for us in it.'

Cat looked at his witch as if she'd lost a brain cell. 'You're forgetting, Aggie. Any money that's going will go to the Wizard.'

The tip of Aggie's nose glowed an angry red. 'Are you saying my bone-feeling is wrong?'

Cat knew his witch! He saw a row coming. 'The town is against us and our home is at stake. This is no time for us to fall out.'

'I don't need you to tell me that! But, if you want, you can tell the broomstick where to take us.'

She only let Cat do this as a treat, and he knew the row was mended.

A few minutes later they landed outside the factory gates.

'Let's have a nosey round!' said Aggie.

As they walked on in, though the day was hot, Cat shivered. Aggie shivered too. Then she stood very still, with her eyes shut.

'Mmmm,' she said, at last.

'Mmmm what? Whatever it is, I don't like it.' Cat shivered again and gripped his tummy.

28

'Does it feel like you've eaten rotten fish?' asked Aggie.

Cat nodded.

'I'm feeling queasy myself. And I know why!' Aggie's tone was deeply serious. 'We're talking Gobtrolls, Cat!'

'Gobtrolls!'

Cat spat out the word as if he couldn't wait to get it out of his mouth.

Gobtrolls had once ruled the world. They had the power to turn blood to stone, and were greatly feared. Then all the people and creatures of the earth, even bad-tempered dragons and ogres, got together to find a spell to destroy the Gobtrolls' power.

At last they found it!

The Gobtrolls knew the game was up. They fled to the woods and burrowed into the earth where the spell couldn't reach them. But with every year that passed, their

30

hatred of all things that lived by
the light of the sun and the moon
had grown.

'Now it's grown
so strong, it's
seeping up through
the earth and
poisoning the air
above,' said
Aggie. 'Come on,
Cat. This is no

31

place to linger. The fence must mark where the wood ended. On the other side, the air is clear.'

As they hurried back through the gates, they saw the Wizard coming towards them, followed by the Wantwichers.

'You're quick on the case, Wiz,'
shouted Aggie. 'But not as quick
as me. The factory's being
spooked by Gobtrolls!'

Cat gave a puzzled frown. The
Wantwichers, too, looked
surprised. It wasn't like Aggie to
do something for nothing.

'Thanks for the tip-off,' said the Wizard.

'Think nothing of it, partner!' Aggie gave a toothy grin. 'I don't remember all the spell for getting rid of Gobtrolls. But I *do* remember it needs a witch and a wizard! You and I are in this together.'

The Mayor turned to the Wizard. 'Is this true, Wesley?'

'You don't have to take my word for it,' said Aggie. 'Fetch the Spell Book, Cat.'

34

Cat fetched the Spell Book from the pot on the end of the broomstick. Quickly Aggie flicked through the pages.

'There! Fix your peepers on that!'

She held up the book for all to see.

SPELL FOR
GETTING RID OF
GOBTROLLS
You will need:
  One Witch.
  One Wizard.
They must each
wear a cloak
woven from
sunbeams and
moonbeams.

SPELL METHOD

1. The Witch and Wizard must enter the Gobtroll-infested area at the time of dusk.

2. Together they must say the Magical Dare. It is a dare no Gobtroll can resist, and they will rise up from the earth.

3. The Witch and Wizard must proceed with Super Magic Wand Waves until the Roar and the Flash.

WARNING: Gobtrolls are as powerful as they are wicked. Any Witch or Wizard who tries to do the spell alone faces certain death by blood-stoning. The same fate awaits all creatures, animal or human, for at least one mile around.

'Like it or not,' chuckled Aggie, 'if you want to work at the factory again, you'll have to pay me as well as the Wizard to magic away the Gobtrolls. There it is, written in black and white!'

'But the Spell Book is old, written before the powers of lasers and even electricity were known. Now, with the aid of technology,' said the Wizard, 'I can perform the spell alone!'

'You wouldn't! You couldn't! You can't!' gasped Aggie.

'I will and I shall and I can!' said the Wizard.

'Then you're not as smart as I thought. We're not talking about getting rid of zits or even rats! But Gobtrolls!'

'I have every confidence in the Wizard,' cut in the Mayor. 'Moreover, why should we pay you as well when we need only pay him?'

'Here! Here! We're with the Wizard!' the Wantwichers shouted.

'No hard feelings, Aggie, I hope,' said the Wizard. 'I'll do the spell at dusk. You're invited to come and watch.'

Aggie's eyes were cold and grim. 'I'll be there invited or not! Before this day and night are done, I feel in my bones disaster will strike you, one and all. And I shall be there to see it!' said Cat's witch Aggie.

'It's almost dusk time,' said Aggie.
'Time we were going. But first –'
She opened her chest of Precious
Things and took out a cloak that
shone and shimmered. 'It's all
sunbeams and moonbeams, Cat. I
know, because I made it myself.'

'But I thought you couldn't sew,'

said Cat. 'You've always said you couldn't.'

'I can't! Unless I want to! And mostly I don't! But never mind that now. When we get there,' went on Aggie, 'you must stay close, so the cloak covers us both. The others will be at the Gobtrolls' mercy. But the cloak will keep us safe.'

'I hope she's right!' thought Cat. But right or wrong, Aggie was his witch. Where she went, he went!

'Let's go!' he said.

When they arrived, the Wizard was already there with the Wantwichers – and a TV crew.

'I've always wanted to be on TV. This is a big moment for me,' he said.

'Your biggest and your last!'
said Aggie.

But she noted the Wizard was
wearing a cloak that shimmered
like her own, and didn't like the
thought that came to her: that the

Wizard had kept some of the old
ways and changed only the ones
that were out of date.

But now day was turning into night.

The Wizard turned to the TV
cameras. 'You're about to see the
spell that will remove the Gobtrolls
from Wantwich forever!'

The Wantwichers cheered as he
strode on through the gates.

'You won't be cheering for
much longer!' said Aggie.

44

'Quiet! The Wizard's about to begin!' said the Mayor.

'I shall begin with the Magical Dare.' Boldly the Wizard's voice bellowed out:

'Gobtrolls evil, Gobtrolls vile,
Gobtrolls wicked and full of bile!
Rise from the earth, into the air,
Show yourselves, Gobtrolls –
IF YOU DARE!'

'Nothing's happened! The Wizard's goofed,' cried little Ali Shah.

But then, a sudden darkness fell.

A loud noise rent the air.

The factory forecourt split in two.

Out leapt creatures that shrieked and howled.

'The Gobtrolls, Cat! Keep close!' said Aggie, wrapping the cloak more tightly around them.

The Gobtrolls
hurled themselves
at the Wizard.
'Yaaaaah!'

'They're turning back! The
cloak's driving them off! Hurrah!'
shouted the Wantwichers.

Once again, the Gobtrolls shrieked.

Slowly, they moved towards the Wizard.

BANG!

The blast was so loud that Aggie blinked.

When she looked again, the Wizard's cloak lay smouldering at his feet.

The Wantwichers gasped in dismay, 'What's happened?'

'I'll tell you what's happened!' said Aggie. 'His cloak was a fake, not real sunbeams and moonbeams. The Gobtrolls have found him out! And that's just the beginning!'

The Gobtrolls were circling around the Wizard. He raised his arms to try to break his way through but they fell to his sides, like stones.

He gave a choked cry. 'Help! Help!'

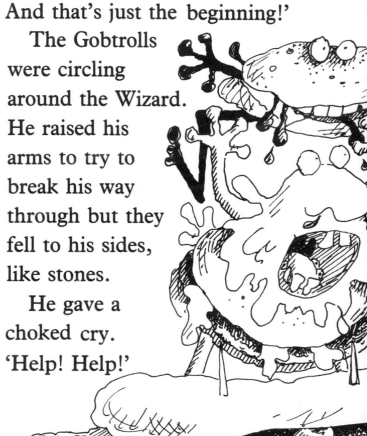

But the TV crew
had already fled.
Now the
Wantwichers
turned to flee.
'I can't move!
I can't lift my legs,'
cried the Mayor.

51

'Nor can I!' the Wantwichers wailed.

'You'll be stone inside and out before much longer! Don't say I didn't warn you!' said Aggie.

'They're coming to get us! Look!' cried little Ali Shah.

The Gobtrolls were heading towards the fence.

'Yaaaaaaaaaaa!'

Cat leapt onto the broomstick.

'We don't want to take any chances. Come on, Aggie!'

'I can't!' said his witch.

Ali Shah began to cry. 'We've had it now! Aggie's been blood-stoned too.'

'Oh no I haven't!' said Aggie. 'My cloak has kept me safe. But for better or worse, you are my people. I can't desert you in your hour of need, which is now, this minute!'

'But –' began Cat.

'But nothing – but I want you safe! Take him home!' At Aggie's

command the broomstick took off,
taking Cat with it.

'Now, Gobtrolls beware! It is I,
Aggie the Witch!'

She ran through the factory
gates. At once the Gobtrolls set
upon her. Her cloak sparked.
Yelping, they drew back. She ran
to the Wizard and put the cloak
round him so it all but covered

them both.

'It'll get your blood flowing again,' she said.

'Yes, I can feel it,' said the Wizard.

'Now, the wand waves! Quickly!'

But the Wizard had no wand, just a laser rod he'd invented.

'Take this.' Aggie broke her wand in two, and gave one half to the Wizard.

'Watch out! They're attacking!' cried Ali Shah.

At once, together, Cat's Witch and the Wizard raised their wands.

UP! DOWN! ROUND!

But the cloak scarcely covered
them. Aggie felt the blood-stoning
power of the Gobtrolls strike. Her
arm dropped to her side. It took
all her effort to raise it. The
Wizard, too, was struggling.

'Keep the wand waves going!
It's life or death!' she urged him.

The wands cut through the air.
UP! DOWN! ROUND!

Sparks flashed forth.

The Gobtrolls staggered in the
blinding light.

Together they turned and fled
towards the split in the earth they
had come from. But the ground
had closed over.

A roar!
A flash!

Of the Gobtrolls, there was no
sign.

Aggie picked up one of the small
pebbles that now lay scattered
about. 'That's all that's left of the
Gobtrolls. They won't hurt you
now. The spell is done!'

59

As the words were spoken, Cat zoomed down beside her. 'I'd never left you, whatever you said. But the broomstick wouldn't come back.'

Aggie gave her toothy grin. 'I magicked it not to, till it was safe. As for you, Wantwichers, your blood will soon de-stone and you'll be yourselves again.'

'I hope not,' said the Mayor. 'I hope we'll never be mean ungrateful selves again. We turned out backs on you, Aggie. But you risked your life to save our town. And didn't ask a penny for it!'

'You're right! I didn't.
Sometimes I surprise myself!' said
Aggie.

'She'll send the bill later,' Cat
put in quickly.

'Name your own price, Aggie.
We'll pay!' the Wantwichers
promised. 'As for you,' they said
to the Wizard, 'we're not paying
you a penny.'

'You goofed, Wizard,' said little Ali Shah.

'Yes, I goofed. I owe you my life, Aggie Witch. Thank you.' The Wizard held out his hand. Aggie took it.

'You're not a bad chap, Wiz. In fact, I wouldn't say "No" to your recipes for rats, bats and spiders.'

Cat looked at his witch in astonishment. 'Synthetic creepy crawlies! You wouldn't use them.'

'Wouldn't I just! I'm not a fuddy-duddy. But I *do* know when to use the real thing. And what I want now is a real cup of tea. You can join me,' she said to the Wizard. 'I'll show you what a real cuppa tastes like.'

'Some other time, Aggie. I've got my packing to do. I've decided to leave Wantwich.'

The Wizard was as good as his word. The next day, he was gone.

'I wonder where he's gone to?' thought Aggie.

One evening, she turned on the TV.

'Owls and asps! I've found him, Cat!'

The Wizard beamed out of the screen.

'I'll be showing you how to make synthetic rats, bats and spiders, with the help of my witch!'

He pressed his control panel's Number One buzzer. A robot clanked on and stood beside him.

'Her name is Aggie. I've called her after a very special witch. Not a robot, but the real thing.'

The robot was neatly dressed and looked very smart.

'But I wouldn't swop you for a robot, Aggie,' said Cat.

'I should think not!' said Cat's witch Aggie.